This book belongs to:

_____

MOUSE
STATION MAP

VERY HIGH
DON'T LOOK
DOWN

IF YOU FIND ANYTHING HEAVY
ASK PIGEONS FOR HELP
(REWARD WITH BREADCRUMBS)

PLATFORM 1

ALWAYS
LOOK
HERE

Please check you have all of your
possessions before leaving the station

← NEARLY THERE →

PLATFORM 2

Any luggage left unattended will be re

⚠ NOISY! BE·EXTRA-CAREFUL

SAFEST TO
GO UNDER

SNACKS

STICKY SPOT
GO AROUND

STOP

STAIRS

DO NOT GO
OUTSIDE

DANGER!

ENTRANCE

THE UNKNOW

BEWARE
BEES →

FLOWER
SHOP

CRUMBS

THIS IS THE MOST
DANGEROUS PART OF
THE STATION

DO
NOT
EAT

YUCK!

YUM!

NO PLACES TO HIDE

COFFEE STAND

BAGUETTE ME NOT

BITTER!
VERY
HOT!

PLATFO

CAREFUL!
MUST
CHECK

LOOK FOR LOST THINGS
AND LUNCH

PLATF

UN MOUSE
OFFICE

TICKETS

DOUBLE CHECK
FOR PASSENGERS
BEFORE GOING
THROUGH HERE

NO STATION MICE ALLOWED

TOILETS

NO STOPPING

STATION WILL BE
NOISY + FULL OF
PASSENGERS

EMERGENCY
EXIT

LOVELY SNACKS

(DO NOT BE SEEN)

BLAH
BLAH
BLAH

BLAH
BLAH
BLAH

ENTRANCE

DANGER!

STICKY

CAFE

HERE BE MONSTERS

CAR PARK

SECRET DOOR TO
DELICIOUSNESS

SAFETY FIRST
REMEMBER...
CHECK FOR PASSENGERS
HURRY & HASTE YE BACK
EYES OPEN
EARS ALERT
SEARCH FOR LOST ITEMS
EXIT THE STATION FLOOR QUICKLY

MICE
MIND
OVER
MATTER

EVERYTHING
IN ITS PLACE
AND A PLACE FOR

THE STATION MICE
Meet your Station Master
ERROL ADAMS
WAKE UP
WAIT FOR STATION TO EMPTY
NIGHT TIME COLLECTION BEGINS
BREAK (SNACKS)
BEDTIME
WAKE UP
BREAKFAST
CLEANING/MAINTENANCE
FREE TIME
NAP BEFORE WORK
LEOPOLD
DAYS OF YORE
GERTIE
OLDEN DAYS
LLOYD
ONCE UPON A TIME
ROSA
WAY BACK WHEN
CLOTHILDE
THE WHISKER WARS
LETTUCE
LONG AGO
GEOFFREY
LATELY
HI NEW GUY! YOUR PICTURE WILL GO HERE

THIS PAPERBACK EDITION PUBLISHED IN GREAT BRITAIN IN 2019
FIRST PUBLISHED IN GREAT BRITAIN IN 2018
BY ANDERSEN PRESS LTD.,
20 Vauxhall Bridge Road, London SW1V 2SA.

HANDLE WITH CARE

PRINTED & BOUND IN CHINA

3 5 7 9 10 8 6 4 2

British Cataloguing In
Publication Data Available

ISBN 978·1·78344·757·2

505

FRAGILE

EDITED BY
Libby Hamilton

ART DIRECTION
Deccy Carrill

LIB:BEC

PASSENGER
k.klugge   496

for all the little mice I know,

BE BRAVE,
BE KIND &
BE YOURSELF

·ISLA·JACKSON·BENJAMIN·
·RAYNA·MICHAEL·RORY·
·CHLOE·LYDIA·

AND
JON
AS ALWAYS

THE STATION MOUSE

MEG McLAREN

Maurice had been told to stay out of sight.

That was the first rule in the Station Mouse Handbook.
And Maurice liked following the rules.

At night, when the station was empty,
it was Maurice's job to collect
all the things left behind that day.

Though sometimes he needed a little help.

Then he slept late into the morning, because of:

RULE 2: A STATION MOUSE MUST
NEVER GO OUT IN THE DAYTIME.

That's when the station is at its busiest.
Passengers, you see, are always rushing
and trains must be caught.

The life of a station mouse
can be a solitary one,

so Maurice liked to
keep himself busy.

In quieter moments he wondered why no one came back for their lost things.

Perhaps the passengers did not want them after all?

But what if he was wrong? What if each lost item was
missed and Maurice could do nothing to help?

Because the most important rule, the one he must never break, was:

**RULE 3:
A STATION MOUSE MUST NEVER APPROACH THE PASSENGERS.**

Not ever.

Now, there's a reason why these rules exist...

AAARGHHH! MOUSE!

Passengers do not like mice.

Maurice would only be safe if he stayed out of sight.

Mice and passengers don't mix.
That was what the handbook
had taught him.

But, for the very first time,
Maurice knew where a lost thing
belonged and that it **was** wanted, after all.

That's when he discovered
that something is only
lost until it is found.

Returning it was
the right thing to do.

Maurice felt better than
he ever had before.

OOH,
THERE
IT IS!

AFTER
IT!

But not for long.

Maurice decided he was going to mind his own business from then on.

The rules were there to protect him.

RIIIINNNG RIIIINNNG RIIIINNNG RIIIINN

Which brings us to the fourth rule:

A station mouse
must never...

hello?

ever...

answer the bell.

Excuse me, I think you dropped your hat.

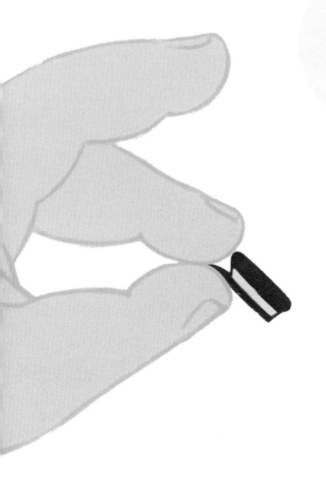

Maurice began to wonder if it was time for a new rule.

Because some passengers **did** like mice. And the rest? Well, they just hadn't got to know him yet.

But that was going to change.

TAKE CARE OF YOUR
STATION MOUSE AND
YOUR STATION MOUSE
WILL TAKE CARE
OF YOU.

LOST AND FOUND

RUN BY MAURICE, YOUR FRIENDLY STATION MOUSE

If you should happen to misplace your luggage or any of your possessions whilst visiting our station, our resident Station Mouse will be happy to help you retrieve them.

If you have any further trouble on your journey or if your luggage has not arrived from your starting destination then Maurice will be happy to contact one of his many national and international colleagues to find it for you.

We are here to help!

Meet your Station Mouse

MAURICE
+ MONTY

MAP

STAY BEHIND THE YELLOW LINE

PLATFORM 2

WHAT IS IT?
NO-ONE KNOWS!

← STILL STICKY GO AROUND

PASSENGERS LIKE TO NAP HERE

WAITING
NAPPING
ROOM
(AND FORGET THINGS)

LOTS OF PASSENGERS TO HELP

THIS IS THE MOST EXCITING PART OF THE STATION

THE STATION STAFF WILL HELP HERE

LOST

AND

FOUND

ALWAYS CHECK THE CORNERS

🕐 BEST VIEW OF THE STATION

HOME
TICKETS

PASSENGERS TO MEET

NO STATION MICE ALLOWED
TOILETS

ENTRANCE

Please check you have all of your possessions before leaving the station. Any luggage left unattended will be removed

+ TAKEN CARE OF UNTIL WE RETURN THEM TO YOU

PLATFORM 1
PLATFORM 2

STAIRS

ENTRANCE

FLOWER SHOP

PLATFORM 3

WAITING ROOM

PLATFORM 4

TICKETS

ENTRANCE

CAR PARK

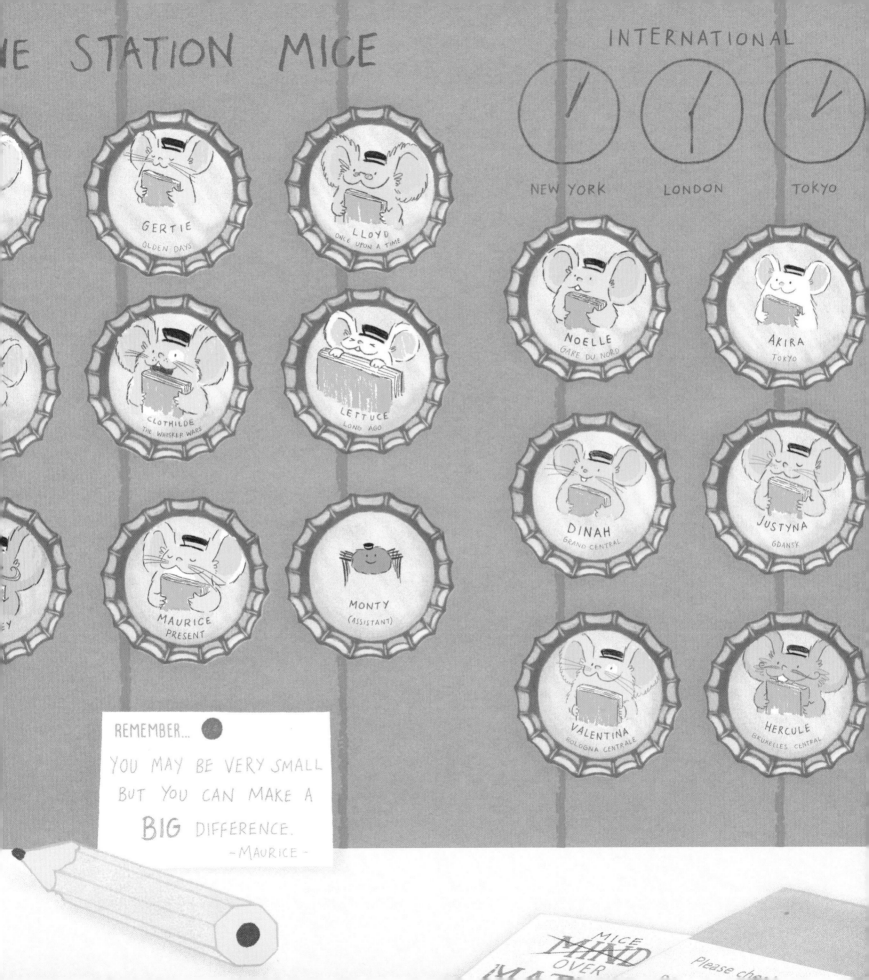

More books by Meg McLaren!